ON THE STAIRS

Julie Hofstrand Larios

illustrated by Mary Hofstrand Cornish

FRONT STREET

Asheville, North Carolina

1999

Printed in Hong Kong

Designed by Virginia Evans

First edition

Library of Congress Cataloging-in-Publication Data

Larios, Julie Hofstrand
On the stairs / Julie Hofstrand Larios: pictures by
Mary Hofstrand Cornish.—1st ed.
p. cm.
Summary: Two mice measure their growth and experiences
as steps, from "first step, rain step" to "tenth step, clock step,
I'm learning to tell time step" to one last light step to glow
in the night.
ISBN 1-886910-34-0 (hardcover: alk. paper)
[1. Growth Fiction. 2. Mice Fiction. 3. Numbers, Ordinal—
Fiction. 4. Counting. 5. Stories in rhyme.] I. Hofstrand,
Mary, ill. II. Title.
PZ8.3.L32540n 1999
99-25625
[E]—dc21   CIP

for
Joshua, Mary & Michael

On the stairs in my house, I play a little game.
Every time I climb the stairs, I give each step a name.

1

First step. Rain step.
Puddle boots are here step.
Yellow coat and yellow hat
and yellow mittens near step.

2

Second step. Measure step.
See how I have grown step.
Now I'm getting oh-so-tall
that I can reach the phone step.

Third step. Window step.
Watch the finches eat step.

Wooden house with birdseed in it for a winter treat step.

Fourth step. Family step.
Photos on the wall step.
Mom and Dad and Sis and me
and Gram when she was small step.

Fifth step. Story step.
Where I sit and read step.
Hidden shelf with all my favorites,
all the books I need step.

6

Sixth step. Mouse step.
Peeking up the stairs step.
See my bed and see my lamp
and see my wicker chair step.

7

Seventh step. Picture step.
Flowers in a frame step.

Some important painter—but I forget his name step.

8

Eighth step. Mirror step.
Where I make strange faces step.

Where I fix my hair if it is sticking out in places step.

9

Ninth step. Drawing step.
Cats and planes and hearts step.
Corkboard on the wall where I
can hang up all my art step.

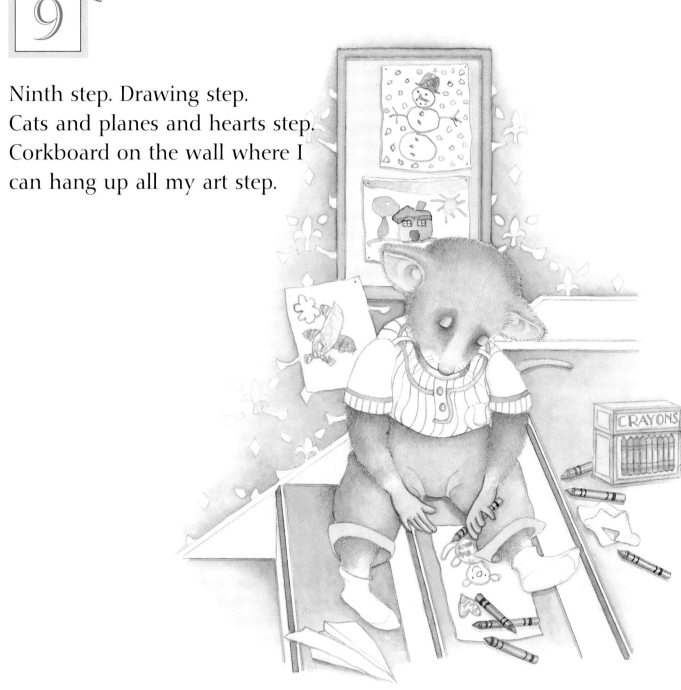

10

Tenth step. Clock step.
I'm learning to tell time step.
Love to hear the ticks and tocks

and listen to the chime step.

11

Eleventh step. Light step.
Glowing in the night step.
Off all day when we are up
and sun is shining bright step.

12

Twelfth step. Top step.
The see where
I have been step.

The now I turn

and go back down

and name them all again step.